WAITING FOR GOOD

A two-act tragicomedy.

M. B. Kaell

Copyright © 2021 Mirella B. Kaell

To Emily & Jack

May the world be at your feet
Its good and your kindness be known
And love find and keep you strong
Today and always.

"At some point, we have to ask ourselves this question. Does one fight evil with good or with evil? It's almost like any progress or invention can be used for good and evil." said LAURA

-M. B. KAELL, WAITING FOR GOOD

CONTENTS

INTRODUCTION

On the evening of the U. S. presidential election, a number of strangers find themselves stuck and threatened, in more ways than one, when a casual metro ride in the San Francisco Bay Area turns awry. As their worlds and convictions collide, will they figure out an exit strategy or perish?

In *Waiting for Good*, the emotions are high, divides are powerful, and opinions are rampant, much like in today's polarized world. The author creates a microcosm of tensions and puts them under a magnifying glass, in a glimpse of time, and under extraordinary circumstances, to examine the psyche and motives of individuals, under a situation of common personal threat and interdependence, to answer some questions about what makes us who we are, and what really matters.

The colorful characters take us on a, sometimes comedic, other times tragic, romantic, and unpredictable roller-coaster ride akin to what life itself, ultimately, is. With thought-provoking patriotic highlights and social commentary on political and societal dilemmas, this quick read is on a mission to attempt to answer some existential and deeper meaning questions both on an individual and collective basis.

The title, *Waiting for Good*, is meant to imply a double-meaning, which suggests impatience in finding the elusive "good," in people and the world, along with the feelings of impatience brought on by seemingly never-ending waiting for a desired result.

PREFACE

I had been haunted, since the late nineties, by this idea of a number of passengers, inconveniently stuck on a BART train and forced to collaborate, in some way, to end their plight. Back then, I spent some two hours, every workday, Monday thru Friday, commuting to work from the East Bay to San Francisco, in the company of a hefty number of strangers, some perfectly groomed and professional, and others, not-so much. In fact, on frequent occasions, I found myself wondering about just this kind of situation, when the train was speeding under the ocean, for some four minutes, each way, in the Transbay Tube, and especially, when it was sometimes stopped there for a few minutes.

Initially, the play was conceived, as a birthday gift idea for my husband. And I started working on it, somewhere around 2014ish, after my challenging recovery from a 2012 New Year's Eve car crash, which put a number of things in deep perspective for me. Yet, it wasn't until the election of 2016 and what followed that helped all of the elements fall into place, and I felt I was able to convey what I had wanted to share with the world, completing what really was the first draft, by the Summer of 2017. Mostly, what inspired me to complete this work, in its current form, has been my ongoing concern with the increasingly divided country and the world, embattled in so many ways, and my nostalgia for more simpler times, when opinions were mostly just opinions, and not necessarily labels, attached to those who voiced them.

I have long been fascinated by the subject of life and death, life's purpose, and the stream of consciousness stylings of Virginia

Woolf, whose works and diary, I studied extensively, while writing my senior thesis in undergraduate school.

If I may, I would like to share a few cherished words, from many moons ago now, written by my professor, Dr. Milani. In a recommendation for admission to a graduate program, he wrote that it was his and a visiting Harvard University scholar's, Dr. Greenblatt's consensus that "Mirella is a brilliant student with great promises for the future." He also wrote: "Mirella has a keen, inquisitive mind"..."She has an insatiable desire to learn and a commendable stamina for rigors of scholarly research. Her Polish background and her command of several languages has provided her with a rare, impressive erudition in the realm of continental literature and theory. Her time in this country has also been used quite efficiently to master not only American literature but some of the more interesting intellectual currents of the past few decades."

In life, my major mantra is leading with empathy and seeking to understand rather than to judge. I had travelled throughout Europe and the United States, quite extensively, and I have lived in three countries and on two continents and learned to speak five languages, which gave me interesting insights into human nature, cultures, and backgrounds. My own life story intersects and coincides with some major events in modern history, which I am tackling, in a soon-to-be published memoir, focusing on the early years and influences that shaped my perception and view of world events and predicaments. Currently, I have several other writing projects in development, including a contemporary mystery-thriller series and another play.

In writing, my goal is to harness the perception of what it is like to be alive and to articulate various nuances of the human experience. Ultimately, whether we convey a certain depth of emotion, lingering thoughts, missing a presence of someone dear, nostalgia for times and people lost, uncertainty of tomorrow, pain of yesterday, breathless ecstasy of elated states of consciousness; whether we are in loss or in love, whatever the current state, writers are just instruments of everyone's quest to capture the essence and meaning of being in this place and time, if only for what really is just a blink of an eye, in the vast endless universe of twinkling stars and deep dark shadows of darkness, rivaled ony by the blackness of the darkest of coals, in which we are the flashing welcome light, like a glimmer of a distant lantern, for a weary vagabond, or a flashing light of a lighthouse, for a ship thought to have been long lost at sea.

Dance, while your feet are still made for dancing. Sing, while your voice still gives music to your soul. Paint, while your fingers still bend the fringes of your soul to pour color and life onto a blank canvass. Daydream, while your mind wonders to places of joy and new-found wonder. Imagine your best day, best life, best hour, best minute, best second, best breath. Feel the wind on your face and wipe tears of joy. Breathe in the clean fresh air after a Spring shower. Linger, on a sunny beach day, to be hypnotized by the waves' rhythmical murmur. Live your life, like it is the privilege.

Yours always.

M. B. Kaell, Pleasanton, CA

CAST OF CHARACTERS

TYRONE, *An African American man in his early 20s*

LAURA, *A Caucasian woman in her early 20s*

MARIA, *A pregnant Mexican American woman in her early 30s*

AHMED, *An Egyptian American man in his late 20s*

SUNIL, *An Indian American in his late 30s*

TOM, *A broad-shouldered Caucasian man in his late 50s*

JAREK, *A Caucasian man in his late 50s*

RENIA, *A Caucasian woman in her late 50s*

SAL, *A Jewish American male in his late 80s*

LINDSEY, *A tall Caucasian businessman in his early 60s*

JACK, *A Filipino American man in his 20s*

JOHNNY, *An Asian American man in his 30s*

HOSTESS, *A woman in her 20s*

THE SCENES OF THE PLAY

ACT 1. BART train, San Francisco Bay Area.

ACT 2. Mexican restaurant, San Francisco Bay Area.

TIME: The present.

ACT I

Scene 1

We are on the BART train, stopped at the Embarcadero station (last stop before the tunnel) headed from San Francisco to the East Bay.

[Several people are sitting in the seats, scattered throughout the train. The spotlight goes on a digital clock on the wall, which says 7:05 p.m. The announcement over the speakers is muffled.]

"This is the West Dublin/Pleasanton train. Please stand clear of the doors. The doors are closing."

[TYRONE runs in, while the doors are closing, holding LAURA'S hand, who is right behind him, and who is holding a plate with a piece of cake on it, in the other hand. Once they make it into the car, the cake flies off the plate and TYRONE and LAURA laugh and giggle. The passengers gasp, smile, and shake their heads. They clean off their clothes, as needed.]

LAURA. *[Embarrassed. To other passengers, with an English accent.]* So sorry. Truly. I apologize, ladies and gentlemen. *[LAURA and TYRONE take their seats.]*

[The sound of the train departing. LINDSEY takes out a newspaper. TOM pops a mint in his mouth and is looking at his phone. The young couple is talking quietly and giggling. Everyone else settles in their seats. The sound of the train speeding up, going faster and faster.]

[After about two minutes, the sound of the explosion can be heard in a distance. The lights blink, then everything goes dark.]

[*The sound of the breaks and the train stopping abruptly, throwing people around for a couple of seconds, and making them scream and react. After a brief buzzing sound, the announcement comes on, muffled, through the speakers.*]

"This is an emergency. Please wait for assistance. Do not exit the train."

[*The announcement repeats one more time, before being cut off. Everyone is reacting, moving in their seats, looking around and out the windows.* MARIA *starts weeping and praying.* TYRONE *and* LAURA *hug each other.*]

TOM. [*Looking around, shaking his head.*] What the f*ck?

SUNIL. [*Loud, with an Indian accent.*] Oh, no! I remember...on the news; they were talking about the imminent terrorist attack in the U.S., on election night. That's tonight!

[TOM *and* JAREK *look at each other. The two men jump on the Middle Eastern-looking man, push him down to the ground, restraining his hands, and start searching him for weapons.*]

AHMED. [*Trying to free himself.*] Man, what are you doing? Let go! I'm a med student at UCSF.

TOM. [*Shouting in* AHMED'S *face.*] Why should I believe you?

AHMED. [*Sarcastically.*] I don't know. Common sense?

SUNIL. [*Stands up. In an Indian accent. With a pleading tone.*] Let him go, please. We need to work together. Let's form a plan to get out of here. In case...you know, we are stuck, and no one comes to rescue us.

[*They reluctantly let go.* AHMED *dusts himself off and walks away from them.*]

TOM. [*Looking around at others.*] Well, with complete lack of survival skills between all of us, good luck to us. [*Looking at*

AHMED.] Unless you were trained out there in Syria or Iraq, in the sand...

LINDSEY. Or here. Like the terrorists from 9/11.

[JAREK *smirks and nods his head in agreement.*]

AHMED. [*Gives them a look of being annoyed. Defensively.*] Look! I've told you; I'm a student. I was born in San Francisco, and I grew up in the Excelsior. My parents are both from Egypt. They owned a liquor store out there.

SUNIL. [*Looking at* LINDSEY.] Actually, those terrorists from 9/11, were mostly from Saudi Arabia, I believe.

LINDSEY. [*With disgust.*] Urgh...It's all the same to me.

TOM. [*Looking at* LINDSEY.] Cut this racist bullshit, man.

LINDSEY. [*Raising his voice.*] Look who's talking. You have just profiled the guy by thinking he was a terrorist, and you suggested he had been trained in the sand, and you call me a racist?

TOM. [*Motioning towards* JAREK, *then looking at* LINDSEY.] We were trying to protect all of us. Even you, asshole!

LINDSEY. [*Gets up and is pointing at* TOM.] Are you calling me an asshole?

TOM. [*Sitting down with one arm stretched on the seat, chin up, looking at* LINDSEY.] As a matter of fact, I am. [*Looking him up and down. With a provocative tone.*] I can tell you're an asshole. What are you gonna do about it, huh, huh?

LINDSEY. [*Motions with his hand in capitulation, as if he is shaking something dirty off of his hand, sitting down.*] Ah, you're not worth it. [*He puts his earbuds on.*]

TOM. [*Gets up. Pointing at* LINDSEY.] Ask me, if I care. Suck my d*ck. [*Louder.*] Let's assess the situation. Well, you two…[*Looking at the young couple.*] What do you know? You're goddamn techies, aren't you? Taking over San Francisco, like it belongs to you. All you know is how to type with your thumbs and be entitled to everything that just fell into your laps. Never mind, your parents killed themselves working hard, day and night, or probably divorced fighting over you. And here you are, the ultimate consumers with your iPhones, iPads, iClouds, and God knows what, while little kids, slaving away to make them for you, can't even kill themselves because they get caught in the nets, in a land far, far away. What do you care? You've got everything on demand, Uber there, Airbnb here, Postmates your twenty-dollar burgers. [*Impassioned.*] Goddamn techies, destroying San Francisco. I hate it now. This used to be my city. It belonged to people who knew what freedom meant, what art meant, expression, really living. Now, it's this pretentious playground for the techies with Whole Foods and Targets on every corner, all for your convenience. And they talk about it like it's their city, forcing artists and real people out on the streets and out of the city. I despise it. [*He shakes his head and grumbles in disgust.*]

TYRONE. [*To* TOM.] Whatever, man. Take it easy. You don't know us. You don't know anything about us. [*He puts his arm around* LAURA. *Her eyes get bigger and bigger.*]

SUNIL. [*Looking at* TOM *and* TYRONE.] Gentlemen, please. Let's be sensible. We have to put our heads together. [*Turning to the young couple.*] Does anyone have any reception?

[TYRONE *and* LAURA *look at their devices but to no avail.*]

TOM. [*Mocking* SUNIL'S *Indian accent.*] Oh, yeah, let's be f*cking sensible. [*Looking up in the direction of security cameras, changing to his American accent.*] Well, government, if you could f*cking hear us now, please send someone to get us the f*ck out of here. [*Louder and louder. Turning to the young couple.*] Maybe you two can smile for your cameras and get them over here quick, before…[*Yelling.*]

We all f*cking die! [*He turns to* JAREK.] What's your story man?

JAREK. Nothing. I just wanna get out of here, man. [*He looks down on his phone in dismay.*]

TOM. No shit!

SUNIL. Well, this may have been an earthquake.

AHMED. [*Looking at* TOM, *makes a mock move towards him.*] Or a terrorist attack.

MARIA. [*Weeping lounder and louder.*]

AHMED. [*With a smirk.*] Maybe North Korea has delivered on its threats and launched a missile.

SUNIL. [*Pensively.*] Let's hope not. In that case, however, we are in the best possible place, underground.

TOM. Not so good. More like...under the ocean. [*Gives* SUNIL *an annoyed look and starts walking towards the back of the car. Tries to open the door.*] Or...maybe some random shit. Some explosion... Damn. We're in the last car. It's locked on both ends, and I don't see another car. It's like... [*Louder. Looking around.*] Hold up! Everybody! Breaking news! No. Excuse me. Fake news. Wait for it. We got disconnected from the rest of this train. We are all alone, out here, in this shit hole! [*Starts walking back towards his seat. Is looking around at everyone and outside the windows. He stops abruptly.*] Whatever it was; we need to make a plan to get the f*ck out of here ourselves.

   [*Everyone is looking down on their devices.*]

SUNIL. [*Looking up from his laptop*] Or at least try.

TOM. [*Sarcastically.*] Or, start drawing names who's gonna eat whom first.

   [MARIA *is weeping louder.*]

TOM. [*Turning to* MARIA, *while walking by her.*] So, you understand

English. [*Smirks and looks at* MARIA *with empathy.*] Don't cry girl. We'll think of something. [*He gives her half a smile, mumbles, and continues to look at* MARIA, *with empathy, who is holding her baby bump.*] Poor girl. [*He sits down, exasperated. Looking around. Sarcastically.*] Well, whatever the hell happens, I hope you voted. It's election night. [*Mumbles.*] This could be domestic terrorism… [*Louder.*] Who do you think will win? Who, here, has a clue? [*He turns to the young couple. They shake their heads. He motions with his head at* LAURA] Of course you don't. Why would you care? She sure doesn't, the Brit.

TYRONE. [*Visibly angry, gets up and makes a move towards* TOM. *He is stopped by* LAURA, *who grabs his arm and asks him to sit down. He remains standing.*] That's enough, man! We do care! All right? We voted. All right? Now what? What are you gonna say? Let's see. I can probably guess, who you voted for…

TOM. [*Gets up from his seat.*] What? Do you want to fight an old man? [*Sits back down. Grumbling. With skepticism.*] She didn't vote.

LINDSEY. [*Abruptly stands up and rips his earphones off. Looking at* TYRONE.] She didn't vote. Don't lie! And if she did…[*Yelling.*] It's illegal!

LAURA. [*Stands up. Addressing everyone.*] Just a minute, let me tell you something! If you must know, I was born here, and I am an American citizen. My parents are both English-American, and we lived in England for a long time, when I was growing up and going to school. We moved back to America, when my parents started working for an American university, and I was starting college. [*Louder.*] I voted. I am 100% legal, and I do care! And I will tell you more. Honestly, I do not understand why there is such an upheaval about someone, possibly not born here, becoming president. I frankly believe that should be changed. I can think of plenty of not-born here Americans, including my father, who would make much better candidates for president than many of the candidates, we had presented to us, in the last couple of elections. It is, as if, being born in America is a single guarantee for patriotism and honor and qualifications. Forgive me for bringing this up, but both the Oklahoma City bomber and the Unabomber had been born here, and they committed acts of terrorism on American soil, against American citizens. Yet, if they had wanted earlier to run for president, and say my father wanted to run for president; they probably would be permitted to do so but not my father, who has a PhD in Government, essentially, Political Science, from Harvard University, among other qualifications, and loves this country. He became an American citizen by choice. He wanted to be American, unlike other people who may take it for granted. It is simply absurd, in my view, in this day and age, to look at where a person was born, over which, the person had absolutely no control, and disqualify them from running for president. There. I said it.

SUNIL. [*Stands up. Animated.*] I agree with you, LAURA. I am an American citizen as well, by choice, and I love this country. I am always 100% aware of what privilege, I have to live here, every day of my life. I never forget, even for a second, how fortunate I am. I also strongly disapprove of the treatment of Native Americans in this country, who are the only true Americans, really, if you want to be technical...[*He makes a praying gesture.*] And there is no reason to get angry now. We are all entitled to our opinions. [*He is briefly distracted by a distant sound of what could be another explosion and flicker of lights.*]

　　　　[*Everyone looks concerned.*]

We...need to...resolve this peacefully. We all want to go home, remember? [*He sits down. Looking around.*] Does anyone have any reception?

　　　　[*There is another distant explosion. The car shakes. Lights flicker. Everyone makes sounds and looks scared.*]

MARIA. [*Screams.*] Oh Dio! No!

TOM. Shit. Not good. Not good at all!

MARIA. [*Weeping uncontrollably now.*]

TOM. No. Don't girl. You will be O.K.

> [TOM *tries to comfort* MARIA. *The young couple cuddles. Everyone adjusts their position, looking around and waiting to see what happens. Everyone is listening, silent for a few seconds. The speaker sounds a short alarm, followed by a muffled announcement.*]

"Thank you for your patience. There has been an emergency; we are working to get to all the passengers. Please stay put. Do not exit the cars. At this time, it is dangerous. Our rescue team is on its way."

> [*The announcement repeats, then cuts off.*]

TOM. [*Points to the speaker. Looking at* MARIA.] See? It's gonna be O.K.

MARIA. [*She gradually slows down her sobbing.*]

TOM. By the way, I'm Tom. What's your name?

MARIA. [*Tentatively.*] Maria.

TOM. O.K. Let's keep calm kids. They're coming to get us. Let's wait and see. [TOM *takes his leather jacket off, and showing it to* MARIA *first, walks over to her and puts it around her arms, with her nod of approval. He then returns to his seat and looks for a way to sit or lie down.*]

AHMED. [*He reaches in his backpack, searches for something and pulls out a large chocolate bar. He offers a piece to* LAURA, *who takes one.* AHMED *takes out a text book and begins to read.*]

LAURA. [*She smiles gently at* AHMED.] Thank you so very much.

SUNIL. [*Opens his laptop.*]

LINDSEY. [*Opens up the newspaper.*]

JAREK. [*He is playing a game on his phone.*]

RENIA. [*She puts her head on JAREK'S shoulder.*]

[BLACKOUT]

[END OF SCENE]

ACT I

We are on the BART train.

[*The spotlight goes on a digital clock on the wall, which now says 9:15 p.m.*]

[*Everyone looks like they are now tired. LINDSEY is loosening up his tie. TOM is laying down on the seats, with his arm covering his eyes. LAURA is resting her head on TYRONE'S shoulder, taking a nap. TYRONE has his headphones on and is listening to music. MARIA is slumped down, leaning her head back on the seat, trying to close her eyes. SUNIL is writing something in a notebook. AHMED is reading a textbook. RENIA is reading a magazine. JAREK is playing a game on his phone.*]

[*The announcement over the speakers comes on, making everyone sit up and listen. Muffled.*]

"This has been an emergency. Please remain on the train. Do not leave the train. It is dangerous to be on the tracks. You could be electrocuted."

TOM. Shit! I swear to God! That's just f*cking great! [*Mockingly.*] Remain on the train because you may die, if you leave. [*Looking up at the speaker.*] Well, we may die, if we stay here, assholes. Wait a minute...Maybe they want us to think that they're coming to rescue us, so we stay put right here, until they gas us or something.

[*There is a movement on a seat that everyone thought was empty.*

10

An older man emerges from between the seats.]

TOM. [*Turning to the older man.*] Wow! Who the hell are you?

SAL. [*Slowly sitting up on the seat. Straightening his clothes.*] I could ask you the same question…

TOM. You mean you slept through the whole thing?

SAL. [*Combing his hair with his hand.*] The whole thing? Wait. First things first. [*Looks around. Bows his head and smirks in the direction of* LAURA, MARIA, *and* RENIA.] I must make myself look presentable for the ladies. [*Turns back to* TOM.] Now, what "thing" are you talking about?

TOM. We're stuck here, brother. This train won't move, and we're on our own. Something exploded and shook, and now we are stuck here, in this car, detached from the rest of the train. They're playing these announcements over the speakers. And there is no live person on the other end.

SAL. Hmm. Sounds fishy. [*He reaches for something in his coat's breast pocket.*]

TOM. Wait. We don't know who you are…Put your hands up! [*He motions to* JAREK *to come over and help him search* SAL. TOM *and* JAREK *run up to* SAL.]

SAL. [*Startled. Slowly puts his hands up.*] What? Do you think, I'm some kind of a terrorist?

TOM. How do I know? Just making sure…All right?

SAL. O.K., if you insist…[*Smirking and winking at* LAURA.] Just be careful where you touch me…I'm old but not dead you know.

TOM. [*Smiling, pats him down.*] All right Casanova. No worries.

SAL. Go for it. This is nothing compared to what I survived.

TOM. Are you a vet?

SAL. Warm but not quite.

TOM. [*Rolling his eyes.*] What? Prison? The great escape? The suspense is killing us. Just tell us. Who knows, maybe we are stuck here, in this shit hole, for good. Nobody will care what you tell us, anyway.

SAL. No, to all of the above. Worse.

TOM. [*Frustrated.*] Damn it! I'm done. Whatever man.

SAL. [*Lowering his voice.*] I survived the Holocaust.

[*Everyone goes silent just looking at SAL with anticipation.*]

TOM. [*Puzzled. Curiously.*] Well, now that you've told us...Tell us how it was. For real.

SAL. [*Gets serious, saddened.*] I was just a kid, you know...Everyone, in my family, was gassed to death.

[*Everyone is silent.*]

JAREK. [*Impassioned.*] I cannot believe these idiots who say it never happened. I've been to Auschwitz. I saw the piles of hair, utensils. I saw the pictures. It's unbelievable that humans can do that to other humans. That much evil is incomprehensible.

SAL. Oh! It happened all right. My family was included with the millions of Jews who went from living healthy, productive lives to being driven to near extinction of the entire race. Plus there were millions of others that were murdered, of many nationalities. We, as humanity, swore this would never happen again, and look at what is happening around the world. Genocide has been and still is rampant around the world. It's horrible. It's incomprehensible, like you said...in one country some twenty million of their own people were killed in the name of power. Let that sink in; it's like an entire population of a country. [*He is looking at JAREK, who stretches out his hand to introduce himself.*]

JAREK. Jarek. [*Shakes* SAL'S *hand.*]

SAL. Sal. [*Louder, looking around.*] Now, let's figure out how to get out of here. I didn't survive that hell to die now.

SUNIL. [*With his hands in a praying gesture, bows down.*] You have a point, sir. We will have to come up with a time-frame, in which, to try to exit this train ourselves, if they do not come. Obviously, we cannot keep on waiting, and sit here forever.

TOM. [*Mockingly. Impatient, shaking his head.*] Ya think?

AHMED. [*Walking up to* TOM.] Hey man, if you're such a know-it-all, why don't you tell us, how we can get out of here and not be just waiting for good.

TOM. [*Sarcastically.*] Why me? You're the one going to med school. You figure it out. [*Turning to the young couple.*] Together with the damn techies.

SUNIL. Let's keep our cool. We cannot turn on one another now. We need each other. [*He looks around, nodding slowly.*] I am Sunil.

[*Everyone else answers with their first name.*]

TOM. [*First huffs to shrug him off and then reconsiders and mumbles with displeasure, under his breath.*] O.K., Mr. "Dalai Lama.' I'm Tom. [*Louder, irritated.*] Oh, give me a break! This is like a seminar.

LINDSEY. [*Sarcastically, looking in* TOM'S *direction.*] Or like an AA meeting..[*Mockingly.*] Hello, my name is LINDSEY, blah blah blah. [*Looking at* SUNIL.] Happy now?

TOM. [*Frustrated. Angrily.*] This whole thing just sucks. Everything is going to hell, this train, our country, the world. You name it. It's all because of the banks and insurance companies. All these rich f*cks getting together, somewhere in Switzerland, where they also stash their money. They're deciding our demise and making billions, while we suffocate...[*Looks around and stops at* LINDSEY, *looking pointedly at him.*] Here, in this shit hole. [*Shakes his head.*]

[LINDSEY *ignores* TOM *or perhaps cannot hear him because of his earbuds.*]

AHMED. [*Annoyed. Mockingly. Looking at* TOM.] Are you always this cynical, or only today, we have the privilege, "professor?"

[*Everyone laughs.*]

TOM. What's that to you, "Taliban?"

AHMED. Easy, "Ku Klux."

[*Everyone gasps.* AHMED *looks at* TOM *with contempt but does not move.*]

SUNIL. [*Gets up and makes a calming down gesture, moving both of his hands in tandem slowly several times.*] Gentelmen! Please.

TYRONE. [*Gets up and turning to* TOM, *loudly.*] That's it man! What's next, are you going to call me a f*cking "N... word?" [LAURA *grabs* TYRONE'S *arm, and he stops in mid-word looking at her. She's pleading with him to sit down but he remains standing.*]
LAURA. [*Pleading with* TYRONE.] Don't. Please.

TOM. Here we go! [*He throws his hands up. Louder and louder.*] Poor blacks. "Black Lives Matter." I've got news for you. "All Lives Matter." And, I don't feel responsible for anything that any ancestors or cops did or do, O.K.? Do I think it's right? Hell no! Do I think the bad cops should be punished? Hell yeah! This may surprise you but I am actually an old hippie, and I believe all of us are equal, black, white, yellow, orange, queer, woman. I can't change what I look like. I know that I'm supposed to be privileged. I know it's easier to be in my skin, for sure, especially these days. But like you, I cannot do anything about that. I am who I am. I'm not racist. I just tell it how it is. [*Looking at* AHMED, *then at* TYRONE. *Leaning his torso forward towards* TYRONE. *Louder.*] Surprised?

TYRONE. [*Stands up.* LAURA *grabs his arm and persuades him to sit down. He makes a gesture with his hand in resignation, shakes his head, and sits down.*] You just don't get it.

LAURA. [*Stands up. Pointing at* TOM.] You have it wrong. African Americans have been oppressed for way too long in this country. It is not the same for them, at all. It's not "All Lives Matter." It is missing the point that is too obvious. Of course, all lives matter. "Black Lives Matter" is about the fact that black people get killed every day, because they're black. There is a fundamental flaw in the basic premise of "All Lives Matter."

TOM. [*Sarcastically.*] Yes, you tell me, young lady, the Brit. Teach me about America, go ahead. It's a little ironic, don't you think? And, no disrespect, but you, definitely, cannot teach me about black America!

TYRONE. [*Stands up, looking pointedly at* TOM, *while touching* LAURA'S *arm and motioning her to sit down.*] Listen man! I bet your mother did not have to worry about you running outside with a toy gun, when you were a kid, or you talking back because running around with a toy gun or talking back to an authority figure might get you killed. [*He spells out the word. Loudly.*] K-I-L-L-E-D! Yeah, killed! For us, it is existential; it's dangerous; it's every day, and almost every situation, in life, can turn tragic. We can be shot walking down the street, at our own home, at a party, leaving a party, getting out of a car, or in the car, anytime, anywhere, all the time, just because we look like someone, or we are presumed to be up to no good. Or we could be suffocated to death with a police officer's knee, begging for our lives, while others are standing-by. You don't think about that, do you?

TOM. [*Annoyed. Silently shakes his head.*]

SUNIL. [*Stands up and makes a praying gesture.*] I beg you, please, back to the situation at hand. Whether we like it or not, we are in this together. So let us be civil.

LAURA. [*She pleads with* TYRONE *to sit down, and he reluctantly does.*]

JAREK. [*Looking at* TOM. *Ignoring* SUNIL.] By the way, if you think there is this conspiracy by the rich and powerful, who are out there to keep us repressed, then turning on one another, is exactly what will make us weak, and we, then, let them win. This here reminds me of the situation, I remember my mother telling stories about, how they had to hide in the basement during World War II, when she was a kid. And they were stuck there, all of them, rich and poor, young and old, healthy and sick, all just trying to survive this one more time, just to be lucky to go on. We can complain all we want but we still want to survive; we still are all in it. Life is precious.

AHMED. [*Looking at* TOM *and* JAREK.] I have a question for you two philosophers. Why being rich is such a bad thing all of a sudden? Huh? [*Louder. Raises his hands.*] This is, after all. [*He stands up. Louder.*] America! [*Impassioned.*] This country was based on building a dream. My father came here because he had a dream of security and prosperity for his family. Now that's somehow evil! I'm studying to be a doctor because I want to make something of myself. I want to help people, and I want to travel, maybe join "Doctors Without Borders" for a couple of years, and then work in private practice, have a family and see them grow and learn and prosper too. Why is that bad? Tell me why we are knocking down prosperity, saying that the millionaires and billionaires are such a bad thing. The truth is, everyone I know, would jump at having a chance to live that kind of life, if only for a day. That is the truth! And, if it were not the truth, all lotteries would go out of business. You can make a positive impact on the world, with money. Some visionary millionaires and billionaires are investing in good causes and giving their fortunes away to improve human condition, by the way.

TYRONE. [TYRONE *and* LAURA *are nodding and smiling.*] Right on, man!

SUNIL. [*Enthusiastically.*] That certainly is the case in my community. Anyone I know, back home in India, loves and adores America because they think money grows on trees here, and that we are all rich, which in many ways, we are. [*He shakes his head.*]

JAREK. [*Laughs and nods his head in agreement.*] So, what's the plan for us to get out of here? Anyone?

TOM. [*Ignores* SUNIL *and* JAREK. *Grumbles and turns to* AHMED. *Louder and louder. Impassioned.*] Oh, please! Nobody is knocking down prosperity. I'm talking about greed. Filthy, uncompromising, immoral, infinitely disgusting greed! In case you all have a short memory. We lost our homes in the great recession. We lost our jobs. We lost are pensions and life savings. Why? Because of greed. Because these f*cks on Wall Street, with politicians in their pockets, got together and came up with a plan to screw us all and ruin us, so they could make more millions. But, you know, that one guy, who got jailed, out of hundreds, if not thousands, of them, those Wall Street crooks?

LAURA. Yes, he got away with it for a long time...

TOM. [*Looking at* LAURA.] Oh yeah, he sure "made-off" with the money, for a while, anyway. But then look how it all ended. A tragedy for so many families, destroying their lives, literally, even causing them to take their own lives. But you know, ultimately, what made this "Made-off guy" possible? It's human greed. Plain and simple. He had promised them crazy returns on their money, and they went for it. And it's bull crap that so many of these guys, really all of them, went unpunished. [*Looking at* TYRONE.] F*ck. If you or I, got caught shoplifting, our asses would be persecuted. Or, better yet, if we got caught with a couple of joints on us, we would be in jail, before weed was legal, that is, maybe for years and years.

TYRONE. [*Serious.*] No man, I'd be dead.

TOM. You've got a point, man... The police brutality is out of control, and I agree, it is towards minorities. I wouldn't want to walk in your shoes. It sucks. It needs to change. Enough is enough. I'm glad to see people get some balls and stand up for what's right. I will vote to end this shit, in a heartbeat. [*Shakes his head.*] Meanwhile, those Wall Street f*cks and corporate CEO money whores, who screwed us, till we couldn't breathe no more. [*Turning to* LAURA *and* MARIA *briefly.*] Sorry ladies. Oh no, they did not go to jail. [*Stands up. He shouts.*] They locked up that one ass-hole! And they bailed out the banks! No, excuse me! We, we, with our hard-earned money! We bailed out the banks! [*He pretends like he's spitting on the ground.*] F*ckers! I tell ya. That's why, we need change. Crooks! Bastards! [*Looking around.*] They are all screwing us, you know? This is why they are rich, and we have nothing, my friends.

LINDSEY. [*Grumbles.*] Cry me river. [*Gets up and starts walking towards* TOM, *raising his voice. He waves a finger at him. Begrudgingly, leaning in TOM'S face.*] I'll tell you something. I'm one of those "Wall Street f*cks" you're talking about.

TOM. [*Leans back and listens intently with an expression of disgust and curiosity on his face.*]

LINDSEY. [*Standing, looking at* TOM. *Impassioned.*] Now. Let me tell you something. Nothing in my life came easy to me. I believe in pulling your own weight. I believe that there is a lot of waste and corruption in our government. And I believe that things need to be shaken up, changed. We're a long way away from real change. Too much big money is tied up in politics. I think, as a society, we need to take care of the poor and the vulnerable, and I also believe that we can do better in not wasting the money and resources like there is no tomorrow.

TOM. [*Mockingly.*] Blah, blah, blah. You're all about greed. I can see right through you, man.

SAL. [*Directed at* TOM, *makes a calming gesture.*] Let the man finish his thought.

LINDSEY. [*Giving* TOM *a look of disapproval.*] Let me tell you a story…I ran away from home at the age of fourteen and never looked back. What I saw and endured no one should have. We were dirt poor, and my father was an abusive alcoholic. He beat the shit out of my mother every night. Last time, I saw him, he was promising to kill both of us, going for his gun. That's when, I pushed him and ran out on the street. He came after me, and once outside, asked me politely to come back in, which I refused and demanded that he bring the gun outside and surrender it. He went back in the house and threw the gun and bullets at my feet. I picked all of it up, and ran, and ran. Later, I called home to make sure my mother was O.K. That was the last time I spoke to my father. My mother passed away from cancer a few years later. I got to visit her in the hospital and spent time with her before she left this world. I worked odd jobs and lived with a friend's family, who let me stay in their garage and helped me get emancipated from my parents. No air-conditioning in the Summer, spotty heating in the Winter. Thankfully, Northern California weather was not too bad. That day, when I ran away, I told myself, I would never be like my father. I would work my ass off and learn the ways of the world, until I knew how to be successful. I put myself through high school and joined the Marines, graduated from college and got a job in the mail room of a large investment company. I became a stock broker and worked my way up to hedge fund manager. I treated my clients with respect and their money with care, and I saw what was going on. Yes, I had made a killing, before the craziness started to go down with the mortgage-backed securities. And I tried to warn of what was going to happen and refused to jump on the band wagon. So yes, Tom, I agree with you, that some of us are assholes that should rot in jail but not all of us. Some of us, just wanted a better life. I can honestly say that I worked hard for everything I have. [*He beats his chest with his fist.*] I earned it. I have a beautiful wife and kids, and I built a bunker for them for this kind of emergency. And I own a collection of guns, and I have a permit to carry, and I go shooting regularly. [*Patting a side of his leg with his right hand, he is waving a finger at* TOM *with his left.* TOM *is leaning away his upper body to distance himself.*]

[*Everyone gasps.* MARIA *starts weeping.*]

LINDSEY. [*Louder and louder.*] And I will tell you, right now! No one is going to take my right to have a gun either! And...[*Shouting.*] Yes, I voted for him! [*He makes a motion, as if dusting off his jacket, and walks back, grumbling, to his seat.*]

TOM. [*Jumps up out of his seat, waving his hands and looking at* LINDSEY'S back. *Shouting.*] You are an asshole! Suck my d*ck!

LINDSEY. [*Turns around and gives* TOM *an angry look.*]

SUNIL. [*Stands up and looking at* TOM *and* LINDSEY, *makes a praying gesture with his hands.*] Gentlemen, please!

LINDSEY. Ah, you're not worth it. [*Annoyed. Sits down.*]

TOM. [*Sitting down, shaking his head, grumbling, regains his composure.*] Damn, I need a cigarette...Riddle me this, Batman. [*Leaning forward and looking directly at* LINDSEY, *ignoring* SUNIL.] If these bat-ass crazy terrorists are after us, you can save us, right?

LINDSEY. [*Uncomfortable, looking around.*] Well...not today. [*Louder, yelling in frustration.*]
This time, I don't have the goddamn gun! I was just supposed to miss traffic and go to this quick stupid meeting; they had asked me to be on the panel for; it was for young entrepreneurs. [*Looking in the direction of* TYRONE *and* LAURA.] You're welcome!

TYRONE. We're screwed. [*Turns to* LAURA, *with a smirk. Sarcastically.*] Sorry, honey.

LAURA. [Giggles.]

SUNIL. It's not funny. Let's hope they are coming to rescue us, and that there are no armed terrorists involved.

TOM. [*Mockingly.*] Yeah, man. Let's hope, and let's pray, maybe. [*Rolling his eyes.*] You know, what I think really sucks is when a football team wins a game and they publicly thank God for their good fortune. I always say: "What about the other team? Doesn't God care about them? Doesn't he want them to win too? What makes our team better than them, in his eyes?" If you ask me, all of our problems start with religion. If it weren't for religion, think how many wars, conflicts and suffering could be avoided. When people claim to do something because of their beliefs, it somehow is supposed be righteous, absolve them of responsibility, common decency; it gives them power over others, even if it's just perceived. Look at all these sexually abused children by priests in the Catholic church, the crusades, the war in the Balkans, any kind of extremism, Northern Ireland's protestants vs. Catholics. It never ends. Just listen to the late George Carlin to open your mind.

AHMED. I think religion is necessary to control people. [LINDSEY *makes a gesture with his finger, pointing at* AHMED, *and nodding in agreement. Looking at* TOM.] Wait... I'm not finished. Religion also helps to sort out, who is who, in society and, besides, it gives people a chance to feel important and heard like nowhere else. It gives them a place, where they can feel safe, understood; where they can gain peace of mind, guidance. And, it gives structure in the family unit, defines the roles of a husband and wife, mother and father and children, and it is supposed to teach us what is right and wrong; what is and is not acceptable.

TOM. So you think religion is...necessary to do all that?

AHMED. I see your point about violence and conflict. I'm just saying that it has a place and purpose; and it is not all bad.

TOM. [*Shrugs his shoulders.*] To me, all of it is bullshit. All religions cause conflict. I know plenty non-religious people who are decent. Speaking of beliefs. I believe, I need a drink.

JAREK. Religion is powerful. When the "Polish Pope" got elected, you know, John Paul II, him and Reagan possibly worked together to help collapse communism. Right honey? You lived this. [*Looking at* RENIA.] Tell them the story.

RENIA. Yes, when the Polish pope was elected; all the Polish people, then living under communist rule, came out to see our Pope, and we sang patriotic songs, and listened to him diplomatically tell us to stand up for what's right; it was incredible. We looked around, and we saw what we had not seen before in a generation; we saw power of conviction, and power in numbers. Then the strikes happened, led by Lech Walesa, and Solidarity emerged. Religion can work for the greater good but it can obviously also inspire those who are up to no good. Also, you know, what's been happening in America that's strange. It's what I call the great American paradox. The few big stores and businesses taking over everywhere, limited selection.

That is what communism was about. Part of what I had thought was so different and fantastic about the West, when I was growing up in the Soviet-influenced Poland, was that choices and freedom were, in my view, almost unlimited in the West. When I made the trip, as a kid, in the late seventies, from Poland and from East to West Berlin, the difference was so stark from grey to color; it was like watching a black and white film all your life, and then seeing the world around you, suddenly turn to color. I could never get that out of my head. The amount of choices, different stores, cafes. I often think of that movie, with Robin Williams, where he is a fresh-off-the-boat immigrant and goes bonkers seeing all the coffee choices in the coffee aisle. [*Chuckles.*]

AHMED. [*Excitedly.*] *Moscow on the Hudson*!

JAREK. [*Smiling.*] That was my wife, when she first went into a Western supermarket. [*He grabs* RENIA'S *hand and kisses it.*] The paradox is that, in America today, we are headed towards fewer choices, monopolies on every front, whether it is the big banks, communications companies, grocery stores, home improvement, coffee houses, you name it, it's here. If they dropped you, on just about any street corner, in any U.S. city, it is fair to say, that there would be a familiar chain coffee house, home improvement store, burger place, gas station, even grocery store or movie theater. These big corporations continue to put pressure on the small business model, which has been the foundation of the U. S. economy, providing some two-thirds of net new jobs and with that, the livelihood and prosperity for millions of Americans, along with innovation and competitiveness. The best part of the free-market economy is innovation and lots and lots of choices for consumers, driven by supply and demand. The point also is that we are limited in our choices, and as our choices are limited, our freedom to choose is constrained.

SUNIL. Yes, absolutely. I was forced to close my small coffee shop, when the big names rolled into my neighborhood. And that forced me to let my two employees go and look for a job at a large tech company myself.

LAURA. [*Whispers something in* TYRONE'S *ear and giggle*s.]

TYRONE. Hold up everyone. We have a situation here. What do we do about, you know.[*Mocking* LAURA'S *English accent.*] Going to the toilet? [*Looking around at all the guys.*] Come on, let's see, if we can pry one of the doors open, so everyone can go outside. Besides, we should try and see, if we can open it, just in case. How about it?

SUNIL. [*Walks towards the sign, with instructions on how to open the door, in an emergency.*] There should be instructions on how to open the emergency doors. [AHMED *and* TYRONE *walk up to the doors.* SUNIL *reads the instructions out loud.*] To open the door manually after the train stops, pull the cover panel away and move the lever in the direction of the arrow. [AHMED *and* TYRONE *open the doors and hold them open.*]

AHMED. [*With a French accent.*] Voila. Mademoiselle.

LAURA. [*With an exaggerated English accent.*] Well, Thank you, gentlemen. Now, I am going to make my "Brexit," if you don't mind. She steps down carefully.

[*Everyone giggles.*]

TYRONE. Be careful, babe. Don't pee on that third rail.

LAURA. [*Laughingly.*] I shan't.

LINDSEY. [*Sarcastically.*] I thought she voted.

TYRONE. [*Angrily.*] Cut it out, man. She did; she's an American citizen.

LINDSEY. [*Shaking his head in disagreement.*]

[MARIA *gets up from her seat and slowly makes her way to the door.*]

TOM. [*Follows* MARIA.] How rude of me. The other young lady would like to join her. Let me help you. I got you. I'll go with and watch you.

[*Everyone giggles.* TOM *gets a bit embarrassed.*]

TOM. I mean I will guard you. Don't worry, I won't look. [*He laughs then exits after* LAURA, *and lends* MARIA *a hand to get out safely.*]

[*About forty seconds go by...Suddenly, there is a sound of another distant explosion, lights flicker and the whole car shakes. Then, a couple of pops can be heard. They can hear* LAURA *and* MARIA *scream.*]

TYRONE. [*Sticks his head outside. The doors start closing and shuts before he can get out. He screams.*] Damn! Laura, Babe! Oh my God! Laura! [*He runs the entire length of the car looking through the windows.*]

SUNIL. Let's open the doors.

[TYRONE *and* JAREK *start prying the doors open.*]

TYRONE. [*To* LINDSEY.] Hey man? We could use some help! [LINDSEY *rolling his eyes.*] Please.

[LINDSEY makes *his way to the doors and helps* SUNIL *and* JAREK *hold them open.* TYRONE *sticks his head out.*] Laura!

LAURA. [*Her voice can be heard close to the doors.*] Stop screaming, love. I'm right here.

TYRONE. Babe, you almost gave me a heart attack.

LAURA. [TYRONE *and* AHMED *help her inside.*] So sorry. I'm back. It's all right. [TYRONE *pulls* LAURA *in and hugs her.* LAURA *and* TYRONE *are embracing.*]

    [*Lights fading.*]

[BLACKOUT]

[END OF SCENE]

[CURTAIN]

ACT I

Scene 3

We are on the BART train.

[EVERYONE *is walking around looking through the windows.*]

TYRONE. [*Sticks his head out and yells out.*] Hey guys, are you O.K.?

TOM. [*From a distance.*] Would you give us a minute?

TYRONE. [AHMED *comes up and holds the doors for* SUNIL, *while* SUNIL *sits down.*] Hey man, what do you think about all this terrorist stuff happening around the world?

AHMED. You don't want to know.

TYRONE. I'm serious. I want to hear your opinion.

AHMED. [*Sarcastically.*] What? On behalf of all my people, I suppose.

TYRONE. You know what I mean, man.

AHMED. [*Lowers his voice.*] That's cool but keep it between us.

TYRONE. You got it.

AHMED. Now, you know, I'm an American, born here to immigrant parents. I think it's partly a product of economics, plus a sum of bad politics, bad policy decisions around the world and hypocrisy. Here we are, the greatest country in the world, where everyone wants to live, bombing the shit out of every little country that somehow strays away from the mold; the mold we want them to fit. Those people there, they have no future, nothing to live for; their countries are either wiped out or dirt poor and with no hope; their families may be killed, misplaced, reduced to nothing. And they know that we meddled in their business. If they wanted to free themselves from their dictators, they could have done it themselves. And oh, somehow the price of human life is different, when we talk about a terrorist attack in the Western World vs. the Middle East, for example. We are appalled, shocked, repeating the number of victims for weeks on end, when they happen here on our soil. While the attacks that happen in the Middle East or Africa, they don't seem as gruesome, or scary, or unacceptable. As long as they are not in our own back yards, and they don't involve American victims, we feel awful but still O.K. about it. We go on with our day. That's messed up. I do not condone any terrorist action or violence, but I am trying to see what gives.

LINDSEY. So, do you think that this justifies terrorism? Because they're making a statement, calling attention to their injustice?

AHMED. [*Annoyed. Turns to* LINDSEY.] I was not talking to you. And that's not what I said. [*Turns back to* TYRONE.] Partly, however, I see that the problem is this disconnect. You know like in one of the European countries, they have ethnic immigrant communities that are so segregated and remote from the main society that the people living there, it seems, are trapped, without any real future to look forward to. We go in the world and occupy and attack and tend to "help," where we have our interests, either strategic or monetary, like oil. Of course, we also help countries around the world and do a lot of charitable and humanitarian work but that is always overshadowed by this heavy hand, we represent out there.

LAURA. If I may, gentlemen? At some point, we have to ask ourselves this question. Does one fight evil with good or with evil? It's almost like any progress or invention can be used for good and evil. Technology, while indispensable now, is a good example. While we use cameras and face recognition technology for security and to track criminals, terrorists are taking advantage of technology and globalization, getting their word out on social media and recruiting people online from all over the world. They are now citizens of many countries and are no longer exclusively of Middle-Eastern descent, and many are, in fact, from English-speaking countries. So much for racial profiling or banning one type of people, which is at its core, so fundamentally wrong, anyway. By the way, there is also so-called domestic terrorism. Remember the Oklahoma City bombing? This is a war of ideologies, of double standards. We have to admit that we have a double standard. I agree with Ahmed. We go out and fight other nations, in the name of profits or interests, in countries, where we have no business being. We bomb other countries, and often there are civilian casualties and humanitarian consequences. I see your point, Ahmed, that when there is a bombing, or an attack in the Middle East, or somewhere else in the world, and the numbers of victims are higher than in any of the attacks or shootings on our soil but the people are not, for the most part, American citizens, somehow that does not seem as gruesome.

TYRONE. Who's to say what life matters more? Remember that movie, The Martian? I thought it showed so clearly that every life matters and is sacred, and we should do everything to try to save a life; even if, it means endangering other lives, and so frequently, using up more resources; it is important to fight for life. Every life matters. Period. And I have to also raise the "Black Lives Matter" to light once more. It has to do with inequality, yes, slavery. That dirty word. That's why this movement carries a heavy burden to equalize what has been stolen from so many, for so long...[*He gets interrupted by the sound of distant shots.*]

LINDSEY. [*Ducks down. Yelling.*] Everybody, stay down!

[*Everyone complies. They hear MARIA scream close to the doors.*]

TYRONE. We have to get Maria and Tom!

LINDSEY. [*Walks up to the doors. To* TYRONE.] Help me!

TYRONE. [*Looks at* LINDSEY *repulsively.*]

LINDSEY. [*Rolling his eyes.*] Please?

TYRONE. [*Makes a move to go help* LINDSEY.]

LINDSEY. [*Sarcastically.*] Excuse me for trying to save your asses!

[LINDSEY *and* TYRONE *crouch down and make their way to the doors. They can hear* TOM *trying to open the doors from the outside. They pry open the doors and help* MARIA *and* TOM *get back inside.*]

TOM. Stay low. I've been hit. Stay low. [*He's holding his arm, which is bleeding.*]

[AHMED *motions to* LAURA, *asking for her scarf.* LAURA *pulls off her scarf and hands it to* AHMED, *who crawls up to* TOM *and ties the scarf above the wound on his arm to stop the bleeding.*]

TOM. I'm O.K. Go, help Maria. I think her water broke.

[*Everyone looks concerned, panicked.*]

MARIA. [*She sits down on a bench, with* RENIA'S *help and begins to moan louder and louder.*] Baby!

LINDSEY. Baby? Ahmed! Aren't you a med student?

AHMED. [*Hesitates.*] Yes, but I'm not...

LINDSEY. No time for butts. She needs your help. You can do it!

TOM. Yes, you can, man. I will help you.

AHMED. [*He helps* MARIA *lie down on the seat with* TOM'S *help.*]

[*Announcement comes on over the speakers.*]

"Attention: Passengers. If you are on the train, please stay put. We are coming to get you. We believe that the situation has been contained. You should be able to send a text message to us with your location. Our computers are down but we can receive your texts at EBART. This announcement will repeat three times. Please listen carefully. Please be patient and do not leave the cars on your own. This is important. Do not try to leave the cars on your own. It may be dangerous for you. We have rescue crews that will be out there to get you but it make take several hours. Stay put. We should be able to get everyone out soon. It may take us overnight to get to you, especially, if you are in or near the Lake Merritt station area or in the Transbay Tube. This concludes this announcement."

LINDSEY. [*Speaking over the announcement, when it repeats.*] This may be an active shooter. What else is "contained?" I will take over now. I have military training. Anyone else? [*He gets negatives from everyone.*] Down on the ground, everyone, now! Stay as close to the ground as possible and as quietly as possible. [*He looks at* MARIA *and* AHMEND.] Except for the baby. We need the baby to scream, right Maria? [*He winks at* MARIA. *The shots are getting closer. He turns to* TOM *and whispers.*]

We all may die but we will try not to, so the baby will live.

[*The sounds of the bullets are getting closer and closer.*]

TOM. [*Yelling.*] Oh, my f*cking God! [*Mockingly.*] "Contained my ass! [*The sounds of the flying bullets are getting closer and closer.*]

LINDSEY. [*Yelling.*] Ahmed, Jarek! Move Maria to the very back of the car. [*He points to the front of the car.*] The shots are coming from there! Stay on the ground.

[AHMED *and* JAREK *lift* MARIA *and carry her to the back of the car.*]

LINDSEY. [*Points to* LAURA.] You too, young lady. [*Points to* JAREK *and* TYRONE.] I need you two. We may need to tackle whoever tries to enter.

JAREK. What if he's shooting at us?

LINDSEY. No going chicken on me now. We'll assume, we can tackle him. Got it?

JAREK. [*He makes a saluting gesture.*] Yes, sir!

LINDSEY. Stay low and quiet behind me. We will have to move around low, even crawl, so we cannot be seen, O.K.? It's important to keep our cool. If we keep our cool, we have a chance. Capisci? I will stand guard in the very front. I will communicate with you what I see. You do not need to peek. If I'm down, Jarek takes over. If he's down, Tyrone. [*The sounds of the shots are getting closer and closer.* MARIA *screams in fear and pain.*]

TYRONE. Shit, man. What if he gets all three of us?

SAL. Then, we're all screwed. Pardon my French.

LINDSEY. Exactly.

SUNIL. Let's not be negative.

TOM. [*Turns to* SUNIL.] Really? Are you for f*cking real? I'm bleeding here. [*Points to his arm.*] I can hear the f*cking bullets and almost feel them on my ass. You may be dying in a minute here. Unreal. [*Shakes his head.*]

SUNIL. I may be. But I also may be not. My chances are 50/50.

TOM. [*Mocking* SUNIL'S *accent.*] My chances are 50/50.

LINDSEY. [*Scoldingly.*] Quiet!

[*The shots slowly subside, then stop. Everyone looks at* LINDSEY.]

LINDSEY. We may be O.K. for a while but let's stay seated on the floor and be as quiet as possible.

AHMED. [*To* MARIA. *Anticipating the baby's imminent birth.*] Breathe. Breathe, breathe, breathe. Hold on. Do not push. I know you want to. You're almost there!

> [LAURA *and* RENIA *are near* MARIA'S *head, reassuring her.*]

LAURA. You're doing great, Maria. The baby is coming.

LINDSEY. [*Suddenly turning to* SUNIL.] Where are you from and how long have you been in this country?

SUNIL. [*Startled; looks uncomfortably at* LINDSEY.]

RENIA. [*Turning to* SUNIL.] You don't have to answer any of that.

SUNIL. I don't mind. I'm from India.

MARIA. [*With pure American accent, intermittently between contractions and breathing.*] You'll all be surprised to know but I was actually born here. Oh, Oooh. Ahhh. Ah. I am an Amer-ic-a-a-n citizen. My mom is from Mexico and my father is from Baltimore. Both are American citizens too. Ouch. Ohhhh. He is a chemist by trade but here he works in construction. He came here originally because his mother had immigrated to America, and she became ill. He took care of her, until she passed away, and met me at the hospital, where I was interning as a nurse. Ooooh! Ahh! So, as you can see, nothing really is, as it appears. [*Breathing hard.*] You know, I get really mad, when I hear this generalized rethoric about Mexican people or Muslims or just immigrants, in general. Ahh. Oooh! Ahh! Who said having babies was easy?

TOM. Don't look at me.

MARIA. Oh, that's right. My mother had me in forty-five minutes, and my brother, in thirty. All people deserve the benefit of the doubt. If they work hard, pay their taxes, and don't commit any crimes, let them have a path to citizenship. Deport the criminals, not honest, hard-working people. Ooooh! Awwwwww. Here it goes!

AHMED. Push! Push! And one more. You're almost there. And breathe, and one more push!

[*The baby is born, lets out a cry, and they hear more shots. TYRONE hands AHMED his jacket, and AHMED wraps the baby in the jacket. LAURA attends to MARIA. AHMED hands the baby to SAL to hold, while he helps MARIA.*]

LINDSEY. We have to get out of here, and we have to go back to the station. It only took about two minutes for the car to get disconnected and get stuck, after we left the last station. The station is towards the back of the car.

[*To AHMED and TYRONE.*]

Get them out safely. You need to hurry. I'm staying behind to distract them.

[*Shots are fired and come closer and closer from the front of the car.*]

[*TYRONE, LAURA and SAL are helping MARIA. SUNIL is holding the baby. Everyone but LINDSEY and TOM are getting out. While they leave the car one by one, intermittent shots are heard in the distance.*]

LINDSEY. [*To TOM.*] Go!

TOM. I'm staying. I'm gonna help you.

LINDSEY. O.K. down on the ground!

[*The sounds of shots are getting closer. Then the lights and sounds slowly fade.*]

[END OF SCENE.]

[BLACKOUT.]

[CURTAIN.]

[15-minute INTERMISSION.]

ACT II

Scene 1

Time: *Three months later.*

*We are at a Mexican Restaurant. Lively music
is playing in the background.*

[*SAL is standing at the hostess' desk.*]

HOSTESS. Would you like to be seated now or do you prefer to wait for your party, sir?

SAL. I'll wait. I'm always early. I'm afraid I'm going to miss something, if I am late...[*He smirks and sits on the bench against the wall.*]

[LAURA *comes through the door with a big smile.*]

LAURA. Sal, you're here already? [*She gives him a peck on the cheek and joyfully squeezes his hands.*]

SAL. Ha! I even beat the Brit to the punch! I happen to firmly believe that if you're on time, you're late. And, If you can be ten minutes late, you can be ten minutes early. Your hands are so warm, my dear.

LAURA. And yours...so cold. Thank you. [*She smiles warmly.*] I know, it's my English heritage. I find it impossible to be late. How have you been getting on?

SAL. You mean since our last reunion?

LAURA. Well, yes.

SAL. Other than having some indigestion, after that last Indian place we went to, last month, in honor of Sunil, just fine, my Dear. Hey, I'm still here, aren't I. I survived the Holocaust, and now this crazy thing.

LAURA. Ha, ha! I'm glad you're O.K. But Oh, you're such a naughty boy. [*Smiling. She wags her finger.*] That food was incredible!

[TYRONE *runs in.*]

TYRONE. Hi Baby! [*He kisses* LAURA *on the cheek.*] And Sir! [*He salutes* SAL.]

SAL. Well, hello, young man!

[LINDSEY *walks in with a bouquet of flowers. His left arm is in a cast and sling.*]

LINDSEY. Well, you guys beat me to it again. Unbelievable. And I am ten minutes early. Let's get a table. Happy Birthday, dear! [*He hands the flowers to* LAURA *and gives her a kiss on the cheek.*]

LAURA. Thank you so much. These are beautiful! [*She does a whirl and a spin with the flowers, out of joy.*]

SAL. Well, Happy Birthday, young lady! What I have for you is a kiss. [*He sticks out his cheek, and she pecks it with a laugh.*]

HOSTESS. Follow me. [*They follow her.*]

[END OF SCENE.]

[BLACKOUT.]

[CURTAIN.]

ACT II

Scene 2

*We are at a Mexican Restaurant. Lively music
is playing in the background.*

[*The* HOSTESS *is taking* SAL, LAURA, TYRONE, *and* LINDSEY
*to their table, with five chairs. They all take their seats. One chair
remains empty.*]

SAL. I still don't know how we made it out of that place. That was incredible.

LAURA. Yes, well, thanks to Lindsey, and his quick thinking and leadership skills.

TYRONE. Yeah, man. [*He puts his hand on* LINDSEY'S *shoulder.*] You never wavered. Thank you! So glad you could join us, finally.

LINDSEY. Don't forget Tom. He was instrumental in getting people out safely. And well, you too, young man. We all had our parts in it. It's great to see you. I tell you. It means a lot. If only everyone made it...

    [AHMED *enters and joins them.*]

AHMED. Happy Birthday, birthday girl! [*He kisses and hugs* LAURA *and hands her a small wrapped gift.*]

LAURA. Thank you so much! Small gifts are the best! [*She marvels at the gift.*]

AHMED. Don't hold your breath. I'm still just a student, you know, not a real doctor. [*Partially covers his mouth and whispers.*] Not yet, anyway.

LINDSEY. Back there, you were as real as they get, my friend. You were awesome. [*He massages his shoulder.*]

AHMED. Gee. Thanks. Coming from you. [*He smiles.*]

LINDSEY. Who would have thunk it.

[*MARIA comes in with JOHNNY and the baby in the stroller. Everyone gets up to greet them and check out the baby. MARIA hands LAURA a gift bag. They exchange kisses and hugs. They get an extra chair and sit down at the table.*]

[*JAREK enters holding a big bouquet of flowers. Everyone greets him. He helps the HOSTESS pull up more chairs.*]

JAREK. Happy Birthday, Laura! [*He hands her the flowers and a gift bag and kisses her on the cheek.*] This is from both of us.

TYRONE. Man, I'm so glad you made it. Where is your better-half though? [*They shake hands and man-hug.*]

JAREK. Are you kidding? I wouldn't miss this for the world. Renia is under the weather, and she did not want to be around the baby, just to be on the safe side. That's my wife; always leads with kindness, thinking of others first.

LAURA. Thank you so much and please give Renia a big hug and kiss from me. I'm so sorry she could not join us.

JAREK. Sure thing. [*LAURA gives him a hug.*] I'll take my kiss now, please. [*He waits for a peck on the cheek from LAURA.*]

LAURA. [*Giggles. She gives JAREK a peck on the cheek.*]

JAREK. [*With a big smile.*] Thank you!

LINDSEY. [*Addressing everyone.*] Remember, how we were sitting there and waiting for someone to rescue us and no one was coming? They just kept telling us to stay put and that someone would come. And we just decided that we would take things into our own hands?

[*Everyone nods in agreement.*]

This is what I'm talking about, when I say that we should all be responsible for our own destiny. We have to take responsibility, whether it is a job we don't like, a relationship that isn't working, our own health and well-
being.

SAL. [*Looking at* LINDSEY.] That is, if we are able to be the masters of our fate. As long as we are talking about the majority of the willing and able population.

LINDSEY. It goes without saying. I do believe in taking care of those in need. I started a charity to help single mothers through difficult times, and I don't like to boast about it. That's not why I do this. I also prefer anonymous donations and to multiple charities.

SAL. That's something, young man. Charity is not the only answer. There is also dignity. Dignity in being able to take care of yourself, unless you cannot do it, for other reasons. Those non-profits and organizations that help people get a fresh start and new wings to fly; those are the winners, in my humble opinion.

LINDSEY. [*Gives a nod of approval to* SAL.] Duly noted.

JAREK. [*Looking at* LINDSEY.] Speaking of being responsible for your health. My wife had to do her own research to find out what was really wrong with her. Like my friend's brother says, who is a doctor, they are all just educated guessers. We should be the ones who really know our bodies. We live in them every day. We should know ,when something changes. It is best to work in tandem with modern medicine, use tests, when needed. And integrated medicine is the way to go.

MARIA. Agreed. However, our society is not entirely ready for it. For decades, the solution was to get a quick prescription and pop a pill for whatever the ailment was. Hence, we have the overuse of antibiotics, anti-depressants, and opioids, just to name a few. Although minds seem to be opening up to new ways of treatment, especially, since the widespread legalization of medical marijuana and use of non-orthodox natural remedies, such as CBD oil and others. If you are into homeopathic medicine, it is often still seen as witchcraft. It's promising to see that some doctors are already actually open to using natural remedies to help the patient, with their overall well-being, even prescribing vacation.

SAL. If it works, why not? I've been on CBD oil for pain, and it does wonders for me. Sometimes, I also won't say no to a puff but only, you know, for company.

[*He smirks and winks. Everyone giggles.*]

JOHNNY. Have you heard of that pseudo doctor, who had built an entire oncology clinic, and conned patients out of all their money, telling them they had some type of blood cancer, falsifying test results and then treating healthy people with chemotherapy just to make a buck?

[*Gasps can be heard. People are shaking their heads.*]

AHMED. That was such a disgrace to my future profession. It was criminal, and I'm so glad they caught him. But that also teaches us to look beyond what is obvious. That just because someone has a great reputation doesn't mean they are above the law. Well, I definitely will have a wholistic approach and will incorporate both homeopathic and conventional medicine into my practice. My goal, as a physician, will be to help people get better and stay in good shape, whether it means getting some special treatment, or going on vacation, or taking a pill, or a combination of all. It all matters. I will definitely not sell out to big pharma to prescribe pills that are not necessary or recommend procedures that should not be performed just to make more money.

LAURA. You say that now, Ahmed. I remember, my friend, who is a doctor, telling me how she was going on an all-expenses paid cruise, paid for by a pharmaceutical company to compensate her for all the prescriptions she had been writing for that particular drug. Now, I know my friend to be a fair and honest person, and I would not want to think that she just wrote prescriptions to get this cruise but incentives are big and people are weak, when it comes to money. We all want things. We all can be really materialistic at times. But it comes down to responsibility. Who should be responsible for all of that moral peril?

TYRONE. Amen. That word "responsibility." It's an important word. Maybe this word is the most important of all words. [*He stands up. Impassioned.*] Because what does it really mean to be a good person? To be good? How can you be good without taking responsibility? This responsibility is different than, let's say blaming the victim, saying they too must be responsible. This is a kind of responsibility that looks beyond what we can see. We need to reach inside of ourselves to find it. It's that sense of doing the right thing, even if no one is there to see you. It's not doing the easy thing, hiding behind an anonymous persona on the Internet, or wearing a hoodie and using the cover of darkness to break into a car and steal things. It means always acting and saying things, as if we are saying them face-to-face to one another, with...

[*He turns his head, looking frightened.*]

Your mama or your granny, or your God, looking over your shoulder, ready to smack you on the back of your head," if you know what I mean?

[*Everyone giggles.*]

TYRONE. [*He continues.*] That's why I also know that the tensions and countless homicides in our black communities cannot all be blamed on police, for example. We need to work together, with

41

each other, and law enforcement to make things work for all of us. I heard of a barber who reaches out to police officers, in his community, by inviting them to be part of the conversations that happen at his business to understand the challenges and share in the triumphs of that what matters to us. That said; The bias is still out there. Racism is still out there. Inequality is still out there. And black men are being targeted, stopped, harassed, chased, and murdered without cause. That has to stop. We all need to be part of the conversation. We all need to acknowledge that the problem is real. It exists. It will not go away by itself. Period. We need responsibility on all fronts to find the real good in all of us.

[*Everyone claps and nods.* TYRONE *takes a bow and sits down.* LAURA *grabs his hand and looks into his eyes, with pride.*]

JAREK. That is so right, Tyrone. Saying it out loud and acknowledging that it exists is step number one. What is important is information too. There is way too much ignorance and still too much segregation in our society. The old folks, you go here. The low-income folks, you go there. The special-ed kids, you go over there. In my opinion, it breeds this kind of mentality; we vs. them. We need to bring back that sense of community, knowing our neighbors, bringing that welcoming casserole or needed bag of groceries, and painting that fence for the old guy on the corner, and by asking questions, having compassion and seeking to understand rather than judge.

[SUNIL *and* JACK *enter.*]

SUNIL. You did not wait for me? [*Rolling his eyes, puts hands on his hips, mocking* TOM, *mocking him. Everyone laughs. He motions with his hands to point to his companion with pride, putting* JACK *on display for everyone to admire.*] This is my boyfriend, Jack. Isn't he just a tart?

[*Everyone giggles.*]

AHMED. Well, you are late, guys. But it's O.K. We haven't ordered yet.

SUNIL. I had to...

LAURA. Enough excuses, just sit down and you and Jack have a Margarita, will you?

[SUNIL *goes over to* LAURA *and wishes her a happy birthday, handing her a gift-wrapped book.*]

[TOM enters, wearing a sling on his right arm; tiptoes behind SUNIL, so he can't see him.]

TOM. [*Mocking* SUNIL'S *accent*] You did not wait for me?

[SUNIL *shakes his head. Everyone laughs.* TOM *comes up to* LAURA *to give her a hug and wish her a happy birthday, handing her a bottle of wine, which she examines carefully.*]

TOM. It is a special wine; our favorite. My wife and I had discovered it, when we had dinner in Carmel for our 2nd or 3rd wedding anniversary at this little Italian eatery, called "Little Napoli." The wine is from Villa Antinori, an Italian, family-owned winery that has been around for hundreds of years. "60 Minutes" had a special on them once.

[*He looks around at everyone, pointing to each one individually.*]

TOM. You had no idea, I was this cultured, did you? Arrr gho..Fu.. [*He looks at the ladies giving him the eye and smiling.*] ..dge yourselves.

[*Everyone laughs. They get an extra chair for him, and he sits down.*]

TYRONE. Tom, do you have any? You know...

TOM. Ah, yes indeed, my friend. And guess what? It's now 100% legal! Finally! I've been saying this for years. Legalize the damn thing already. The demand will go down immediately and this will put all the drug dealers out of business. All the countries that have done it, are glad they did. Legalizing dope takes care of so many problems. Why are our prisons so overcrowded? [*Looking at* TYRONE.] Sorry, man. You got me started. And do you know how to end that heroin epidemic? Same thing. Just legalize it. In certain countries, they have programs to help the addicts; they give them clean needles, help them detox and get on with their lives, without retribution. This is what we need. We also need to have more help for people to beat their addiction and not slapping them on the hand, telling them that they're doing something wrong. You want more jobs, train more mental health professionals, and pay them well. The possibility of getting real help will give more people the courage to get clean. And by the way, legalizing this stuff, will help get the corrupt cops off the streets.

JAREK. Amen, man. [*He gives* TOM *an air* five.]

LAURA. [*Turns to* LINDSEY *and* TOM.] Since we now have both of you here, I've been dying to hear, how you pulled that off.

TOM. [*Points to* LINDSEY, *giving him the "go ahead" sign.*] Ladies first!

[*Everyone giggles.*]

LINDSEY. All right, all right, asshole. [*He looks at* TOM *with disgust.*]

LAURA. [*Rolling her eyes.*] Gentlemen, please!

[*Everyone smiles.*]

LINDSEY. So, after we had gotten everyone out through the back door, we stayed laying low to the ground. I figured they were trying to find a place to barricade themselves, maybe take hostages, and I wanted to stall them, so they would not harm everyone. We wanted to surprise them and knock them down, when they entered the car, make them think no one was left inside. That's why we kept that one door opened a crack to lure them to it. Remember, Tom had already been shot in the arm, so I knew it would be difficult. But, honestly, as much as I hate to say it, I had known all along that he would be the one to help me. [*Looking at* TOM, *semi-admiringly and semi-annoyed.*]

[*Everyone gasps, smiles, and claps.* LINDSEY *smirks and motions with his hands to quiet everyone.*]

TOM. [*Throws back imaginary long-hair, as a woman would. In a high voice, with contention.*] Now you tell me.

[*Everyone laughs.*]

LINDSEY. [*Playing along.*] Don't let it go to your pretty little head, now.

[*Everyone laughs.*]

LAURA. [*To* LINDSEY, *excitedly.*] Do tell what happened next.

LINDSEY. [*Getting serious.*] And sure enough, they came right to the door. We could hear them speaking to each other but we had no clue what they were saying. We figured they wanted to check if anyone was inside. That's when the one guy entered. I was closest to the door, so I grabbed him by his legs, as hard as I could, and pulled him down immediately. Tom knocked him out with my laptop, took his weapon, and handed it to me, once I tied the guy's hands behind his back with my tie. The guy outside started shooting at the car. We could hear the shots getting closer, and he was hitting the car. We retreated back. I knelt down in front of Tom, waiting for the bastard to climb in. He peeked in from the right and was aiming a handgun at Tom; I leaped and shielded Tom, while I was firing at the guy. That's when I got hit in the left arm. I proceeded to shoot at the guy with my right hand and was able to get him in the right shoulder, which knocked him down, and he fell out of the car. I got up and shot at him several times, while he was already outside. We could hear the sirens getting closer. That's when I passed out.

45

[*He motions with his hand and looks at* TOM *to continue the story*.]

TOM. You sure were, passed out, man! I didn't know, if any more of those motherf*ckers, pardon my French, were out there to get us but I pulled Lindsey away from the door and wrapped his fancy cashmere scarf around his arm to stop the bleeding. Then, I waited for a while before peeking out to check out the scene. I saw the dead guy's body slumped outside. Then, I waited and listened. I could hear the S.W.A.T. team approaching. I heard them call out on the loud speaker: "Drop your weapons and come out slowly, with your hands up!" Lindsey was still passed out, and so was the tied-up bastard. I yelled out, "Don't shoot! Civilians hurt here. One hit perpetrator outside; one held inside!" They approached slowly, and came in to help us. That's it. We were pulled out and transported to the hospital, where the awesome doctors and nurses worked on us.

[*Everyone gasps in admiration.*]

LINDSEY. [*Looking at* TOM, *with tears in his eyes.*] Man, you saved my life! Thank you.

TOM. [*Tearing up. Voice breaking up. Pointing at* LINDSEY!] Brother! And you, mine. You, da man, man! You da man!

[*They embrace and hug each other, carefully, and somewhat awkwardly, avoiding their opposite slinged arms.*]

LAURA. And you two, saved all of us! We love you. Thank you!
[*Everyone stands up and applauds, tears of joy flowing. They start hugging and kissing each other.*]

AHMED. And they weren't even terrorists, were they?

SUNIL. Not at all. Just bank-robbers on the run. [*Shaking his head.*]

[*Everyone talks amongst themselves.*]

MARIA. [*To* AHMED.] And you, saved my life and my baby's life, for sure. So thank you, Ahmed! [*Blowing him air kisses.*]

[*Addressing everyone.*]

You know, when you think about it, we all can get along just fine, when we face common danger. In other situations, we do as well. Look what happened with healthcare reform. When people got faced with the prospect of their own healthcare being taken away from them or their families, regardless of the party affiliation, they stood up to power at the townhall meetings and voiced their opinions and ended up being heard. We need to see the common good, over politics, which is driven by money, and essentially supported by the people who have both, power and money, and are interested in keeping both, and who do not, necessarily, have everyone's best interest at heart but rather their own. [*Looking around at everyone.*] When I worked on my thesis in grad school, I was interested in learning how politics affects human behavior. I conducted a lot of interviews and observed individuals of different party affiliations and their different levels of willingness to listen and to understand one another. In politics, we have to admit to ourselves, that we are willing to turn the blind eye to some questionable things our favorite candidate may be doing, excusing their behavior, and we naturally jump on every chance to criticize the opposing candidates. Perhaps it's a survival tactic, and nobody is perfect but it misses out on the fundamental principal that we should all focus on, and that is... [*She looks around to make sure she has everyone's full attention.*] The truth. What is the truth? And how are we going to get to know it, if all we care about is our side and being right, and our point-of-view; politics over country? Part of it is lack of responsibility for anything anymore, like Tyrone said, especially our words. With the anonymity of the INTERNET, words are thrown out without much consideration or consequence, and that only leads us to be more divided than ever. [*She shakes her head in disbelief and frustration.*]

SAL. I agree, entirely, my dear. What really gets me, is how quickly we become complacent. All the advances in technology that are so dramatic happened mostly within the one hundred year window, or so. Think about what we did not have before, and what we know now, and how little we know of what is still out there. Just take a look at the stars. We are just specs of dust in the vast universe. All our struggles, triumphs, and the very existence on this planet are temporary. Then, it really depends what you believe. Some think, it's safe to believe that there is something beyond this physical existence, and believe just in case. Others are firmly convinced of the higher power, spiritual activity, other dimensions. Still others do not believe any of this and claim they cannot believe in that, which they cannot see. We should ask ourselves this question. If we cannot see it, does it mean it does not exist? For example, we cannot really see love, yet we know it exists, don't we?

[*He smiles and raises the glass, looking at* LAURA *and* TYRONE, *and they raise their glasses and smile back.*]

And the power of the mind is quite infinite, and it can carry us through unimaginable harm and obstacles. I am here to tell you, that what you set out in your mind, will happen. If I did not know how to control what was in my mind, even as a youngster, I could have never survived the horrors of the concentration camp and the war. Well, one thing is for sure. If we continue on this path, it will only lead us to destruction. We need to talk to one another. And more importantly, listen to one another. And even most importantly, be honest with ourselves, and be willing to admit to our mistakes, to see all sides of the story. Make a point of knowing someone different than us. Ultimately coming together to find what is most important: health, peace, family, and prosperity. The things we all should and do care about. My dear friends, vote. Every time. All the time. But I digress...[*Raising his glass for a toast.*] Here's to us! [*Pointing his glass up and smiling, looking around at everyone.*]

[*Everyone participates in the toast.*]

JAREK. Maria, you brought up an interesting point about the truth. These days, each side is calling the other side's news, "Fake News." It matters what you listen to, and what you believe. My wife told me about state-owned media, under Communism, as I was born in Chicago to Polish parents, I had never experienced that. Growing up in Poland in those days, she had learned to question everything and everyone. As a young kid her family was teaching her that it was all propaganda. She remembers hovering with her parents over a radio, listening to Radio Free Europe, being careful so the neighbors would not hear it because you could not trust anyone. Back in the fifties, even before her time, a neighbor, co-worker, anyone could turn you in, and you could be incarcerated, or worse, sent off to a labor camp, somewhere in Siberia; and often disappear without a trace. She also gets frustrated, when people throw out terms like socialism and communism, without taking care to really understand what they mean. Striving for common good and taking care of those, in or midst, who need a helping hand, is not communism or socialism; it is showing empathy and doing our part, on a community level. Here is the big problem in our society. How do we know the truth? If wealthy people, companies and organizations pay to elect officials, who then pass laws based on their interests, how can we ever get to the truth and have things work for the common good? [*Looking at everyone, louder, with a sigh of frustration.*] How do we get to the good? How do we get to it?

TOM. Well first, we have to get the f*cking, [*looking at LAURA and MARIA*] sorry ladies, money out of politics. That's number one. As citizens, individually, we should be able to donate to the best candidate. Period. Twenty-seven-dollars, or so, per person, times millions and millions of us. No Super PAC's, no lobbyists.

TYRONE. For sure. We have to be able to support our candidates. We need to all have a voice. Why can't they make everyone vote, just like we all have to have a driver's license to drive? To be an adult, you should become informed about how things we vote on, affect us; to be an adult should be to vote. Voting should be mandatory. Voting is a right and a privilege. People suffered; were tortured, incarcerated, died, just so we could vote. Let that sink in for a minute. [*Looking around, impassioned, louder and louder.*] There are plenty of people who want us to take voting lightly. That's why they make it difficult to register and to vote, especially for the minorities. With all the technology we have now, it should not be a problem. We can send drones half-way around the world and kill people on demand, while watching live on camera; we can sign on-to our stupid smart phones, with our thumb-print to ensure our identity, so don't tell me that we cannot ensure the same for voting! And logistically, make it easy already. We can magically cast millions of votes for a contestant on a TV show, so why can't we apply this to voting for candidates? Why can't we vote on a weekend? Extend the timing. Make it online, make it mobile, like an app on the smart phone. And you turn eighteen, and you are in your right mind...[*Jokingly.*] We hope.

[*Everyone giggles.*]

TYRONE. You vote, before you can legally drink. Make voting cool. That's it. End of story.

AHMED. Done. I'll drink to that! Cheers!

[*Everyone raises their glasses to drink.*]

LAURA. [*Looking admiringly at* TYRONE, *stands up. Rings a glass with a fork.*] May I have everyone's attention, please?
[*Everyone quiets down and looks at* LAURA.]

I wrote a few words that I want to share with you, if I may?

SUNIL. Please do.

LAURA. [*Reading from a piece of paper.*] I think that from our shared experience of pure horror and fear, we have learned that we are more alike than we are not. That things that really matter are not material. That love is always just around the corner. That empathy and kindness are behind just one smile. That we cannot understand others with a closed heart. That everyone of us has a struggle. That we can count on one another because a friend is just one handshake away from a stranger. I hope we remember and tell everyone we love and know that, just like in the face of adversity, we can be human first, American second, and then Democrat, [*She pauses and looks around for reactions, motioning everyone to wait.*] Independent, Libertarian, Republican,...or any other, [*Looking around at everyone.*] in alphabetical order, because the outline of good is already here, as long as, we fill in all the blanks ourselves. Ultimately, with some outlier extreme exceptions, we all want the very same things for ourselves and our loved ones, like health, love, security, prosperity and, of course, happiness. Thank you. It's such a great honor to be in your company. [*She raises her glass.*] Together, and not apart, we make this country great. Here's to us!

[*Everyone raises their glasses for a toast. and says.*]

To us!

[*Everyone nods, and applauds.*]

TYRONE. [*Gets up from the table, gets down on one knee, in front of LAURA, and opens a little box.*] Laura, my sweet, incredible woman. Would you marry me?

LAURA. [*Covers her face with her hands in excitement and is speechless for a moment. She exclaims.*] Oh my God!

TYRONE. [*Puzzled, with anticipation in his eyes.*] Is that a "Yes?"

LAURA. [*Yells.*] Yes! Yes!

TYRONE. [*In a serious tone.*] But not before...you answer this question.

[LAURA *looks stunned. Everyone gasps then is silent.*]

TYRONE. [*Looking into* LAURA'S *eyes.*] Why do you want to marry me?

LAURA. [*Looks* into TYRONE'S eyes, *putting her right hand on her heart and says.*] Well, my darling,...[*She looks around at everyone, nodding her head.*] For your money, of course!

> [*Everyone bursts into laughter.*]

TYRONE. [*He looks around at everyone, shaking his head.*] Well then, I've got news for you, young lady!

> [*Everyone laughs.* LAURA'S *eyes well up with tears, as she grabs both of TYRONE's hands and gets serious, looking into them again.*]

LAURA. Because...when I close my eyes to go to sleep, I cannot fall asleep, without giving you a kiss first. And because every day, I am curious to keep uncovering every little thing that makes you who you are. And because you are so good to me; always. And because you're just so kind and... one-of-a-kind. And I can't wait for you to get home, every day, because you enrich every minute of my life, without going anywhere.

> [TYRONE *grabs her, kisses her, and swirls her around. Everyone claps and screams out of joy.*]

LAURA. Wait. That's not all. [*She looks around at everyone, holding* TYRONE'S *hand.*] Ladies and gentlemen, we have an announcement to make...

> [*Everyone looks at* LAURA, *with great anticipation.*]

We are going to have a baby!

> [*Everyone screams out.*]

Congratulations!

TYRONE. [*With a big smile.*] And, boy or girl, we are going to name him or her...

LAURA. Wait for it... [*She is looking at* LINDSEY *and then around at everyone. Then she grabs* TYRONE'S *hand, and raising both arms, exclaims!*]

AMERICA!

> [*Lights are dimmed, everyone freezes and is silent, the spotlight is on* TYRONE, *as he starts reciting, and he walks up to the front of the stage, looking out into the audience.*]

TYRONE. [*He stands in the center of the stage and points at the audience, then back at himself and out further above the audience.*] We're all American, it's you, it's me. Ocean to ocean, we are America; something to see. We're all American, we're proud; we're fire and lace, we are proof that we're all part of the same, the one and only, the human race. [*He does not move.*]

> [*The spotlight goes to* LAURA, *who walks up to join* TYRONE *at the front* of the stage.]

LAURA. We're all American, it's you, it's me. Ocean to ocean, we are America; something to see. We stand united for love, for peace, for family, friendship, basketball, baseball, and many different creeds. [*She grabs* TYRONE'S *right hand, and they do not move.*]

> [*The spotlight goes to* JACK, *who stands up and walks up to stand next to* LAURA.]

JACK. We're all American, it's you, it's me. Ocean to ocean, we are America; something to see. Picnics and tailgates, birthdays, movie nights, Shakespeare in the park, fireworks, carefree Summer rides. [*He grabs* LAURA'S *hand, and they do not move.*]

> [*The spotlight goes to* SAL, *who stands up and walks up to stand next to* TYRONE.]

SAL. We're all American, it's you, it's me. Ocean to ocean, we are America; something to see. We stand on the shoulders of heroes, who suffered, who died, fighting for the country, for freedom to rise, for equality, for women and men to sit as we please, to believe and love and worship with ease. [*He grabs* TYRONE'S *hand, and they do not move.*]

[*The spotlight goes to* SUNIL, *who stands up and walks up to stand next to* SAL.]

SUNIL. We're the envy of the world, where neighbors unite. We believe differently, with no need to fight. We don't look alike. We love the same stuff. We love as we please, and protest, and vote, and together, we care for our plight. [*He grabs* SAL'S *hand, and they do not move.*]

[*The spotlight goes to* MARIA, *who stands up and walks up to stand next to* JACK.]

MARIA. We're all American, it's you, it's me. Ocean to ocean, we are America; something to see. We're all American to stay and to be, as we are beautiful and kind, come and see. We won't turn you away, if you need us, we're here. [*She grabs* JACK'S *hand, and they do not move.*]

[*The spotlight goes to* AHMED, *who stands up and walks up to stand next to* SUNIL.]

AHMED. We're all American, it's you, it's me. Ocean to ocean, we are America; something to see. Don't think, for a minute, we're ready to quit, this experiment in prosperity and freedom, or to give up our dreams. [*He grabs* SUNIL'S *hand, and they do not move.*]

[*The spotlight goes to* TOM, *who stands up and walks up to stand next to* MARIA.]

TOM. We're all American, it's you, it's me. Ocean to ocean, we are America; something to see.
American heroes will protect and guard what is uniquely ours, so stand back, don't attack, as we are ready to fight. Fight with love, fight with might, understanding everyone's plight. No hate, no fear, no enemies; love is near. [*He grabs* MARIA'S *hand, and they do*

not move.]

[*The spotlight goes to* LINDSEY, *who stands up and walks up to stand next to* AHMED.]

LINDSEY. We're all American, it's you, it's me. Ocean to ocean, we are America; something to see. We care for each other, those with and without. We love the sick, the lonely, with might. Our most cherished export is this love and care, we are as we seem, we don't just sit from afar and stare. [*He grabs* AHMED'S *hand, and they do not move.*]

[*Other members of the cast walk up to the front.*]

[*Everyone together.*]

We're all American, it's you, it's me. Ocean to ocean, we are America; something to see.

[*Lights are dimmed. The spotlight is on* TOM.]

TOM. We're all American, it's you, it's me. Ocean to ocean, we are America; something to see. [*Pointing out to the audience, and then to himself.*] And now it's up to you and me that being American is, and always will remain, something to aspire to be.

[*The lights come back on.*]

[*Everyone on stage joins hands and takes a bow. Everyone takes two steps back and takes one more bow.*]

[BLACKOUT.]

[CURTAIN.]

[*A large image of the American Flag is displayed on the curtain.*]

[END OF SCENE.]

THE END.

ACKNOWLEDGMENTS

We really do not exist, without those who care about us. Our existence only matters, if those who really care and know all that makes us unique, what makes us tick, what makes us sad, happy, awkward, broken, accomplished, appreciate our presence. No one remembers the seemingly mundane routines of our daily lives, and even if we think of ourselves as able and independent human beings, the truth is that not one notable accomplishment would be possible, in our lives, without people, who are there to not just inspire us, build our confidence, lend a helping hand or word of advice, and sometimes, pull us out of the darkest places but also just simply cook or order our favorite meal, throw a blanket on us, when we are working late into the night and pass out on the couch, or pick up a treat, when we need it most. They can be family members, friends, colleagues, teachers, and neighbors. The biggest difference can be just an encouraging word, smile, or enthusiastic reaction to what is important to us that will allow us to keep working and believing and persevering.

In my life, there are and were so many people that made an impact on me, encouraged me, believed in me, and through it all, helped make this work possible. And taking a risk of not remembering every person, I want to name them here, with my biggest gratitude, from the bottom of my heart, thank you. I love you all.

Mom
Ron & Nick Kaell
Piotr & Kristin Tomasik & extended family
The Kaell Family

The Ochman Family
Denise & Steve Freedman & extended family
Renata Adrianek & extended family
Marek Biernacinski & extended family
Melissa Rothermel Biernacinski
The Benziger Family
The Clark Family
Gosia & Robert Zygadlo & extended family
Dad
Nissa Nack
Kathy Farkas Bene
Dr. Jean Marie Novak
Marjory Lualhati
James "Quixote" Underwood
Manon & Coco Underwood
Jim Underwood
Ania Omski & Raj Talwar & extended family
Toni Heyneker
Curt Morgan
Eleanor Hiles
Michael Girardin
Christin Noel
Matt Crisp
Barbara Brady
Andre & Courtney Welsh
Chioke Jelani Clanton
Geoffrey & Karen Lower
Magdalena & Angelo Modica
Barbara Dyszynski & Richard Smolen
Kathy Hougen Rothermel
Kimberly Yegge
Tomas Mielnicki
Peter Filipowski
Robert Zmrzli
Dr. Abbas Milani
Dr. Ardavan "Ardy" Davaran

Dr. Marc Wolterbeek
Professor Kevin Maxwell
Dr. Scott Klein

ABOUT THE AUTHOR

M. B. Kaell

Mirella B. Kaell, nom de plume, M. B. Kaell, is a poet, writer, and author of the new stage play Waiting for Good. She believes that her life's purpose has largely been accomplished, since she is now a proud babcia of two amazing humans, Emily and Jack. And, albeit the seemingly never-ending lockdown rollercoaster ride, she feels like she got to stop and exhale for a moment, now that her alarming desire to address some major issues, arising and brewing in the world, has been fulfilled,  when she put pen to paper and completed this short read, in the works, since probably 2014ish.

Mirella holds a Bachelor of Arts degree in English, with a minor in computer science, and her Master of Science degree is in Psychology. She has many interests and believes in lifelong learning and pursuing what you love, with passion and focus, regardless of your place on the timeline of life. She and her husband reside in the San Francisco Bay Area.

www.ingramcontent.com/pod-product-compliance
Lightning Source LLC
Chambersburg PA
CBHW070646130626
46555CB00006B/2729